Guardian

Guardian

A DAUGHTER OF ZYANYA NOVELLA

Morgan J. Muir

This is a work of fiction. Names, characters, places, and incidents either are the product of the author's imagination or are used fictitiously. Any resemblance to actual persons, living or dead, events, or locales is entirely coincidental.

Copyright © 2020 by Morgan J. Muir

All rights reserved. No part of this work may be reproduced or used in any manner without written permission of the copyright owner except for the use of quotations in a book review.

Cover & book design by Morgan J. Muir
www.Morganjmuir.com
Cover art by Dimitar Spasov
www.artstation.com/stretch

ISBN-13: 978-1-7338906-5-6

ALSO BY MORGAN J. MUIR

Daughter of Zyanya
Aura of Dawn – a Prequel
Amaranth Dawn – Book 1
Aeonian Dreams – Book 2
Abiding Destiny – Book 3

Short Stories
Nadir: A short story of Motherhood
Control: A short story of Courage
Burdened: A short story of Choice
Heartfelt: A short story of Loyalty
Nameless: A short story of Hope

Paws: Sheltie Stories (graphic novels)
Paw Prints
Paws of Power (*forthcoming*)
Path of Paws (*forthcoming*)

Available at Amazon.com

1

SUMMER 1722 – GUARJIRO PENINSULA, NORTH of MARACAIBO

THE GREEN AND RED crickets chirruped in the fading sunlight, leaping across the dusty path. Ayelen's hand held her husband's as they walked along the wild field of grass, her brother beside them. A herd of goats approached, guided by a young girl and her toddling little sister. The toddler stopped beside Ayelen, tugging at her patterned skirt.

"You've been caught," Ciro said with a smile, and Ayelen dropped his hand to scoop up the toddler.

"She just wants a treat," the older sister said, annoyed at the delay.

"Is that what you're after, little Muusa?" Ayelen asked the toddler, who grinned, then hid her face in Ayelen's shoulder. "Maybe you'd better ask Ciro if he's got anything."

"I don't know…" Ciro hedged, and Ayelen smiled as he reached into his pouch. "I'm not sure I could give treats to children without faces."

Muusa immediately faced him and stuck out her tongue. With a grin, Ciro handed over the small sugar cube, and Ayelen set down the toddler.

"And one for your sister, too," Ciro whispered, handing over another before the girl ran to catch up with the goats.

"And hurry home!" Ayelen called out after them. "You shouldn't be out after sunset."

Ayelen glanced at her husband and smiled. The way he watched the village children warmed her heart. One day, they would have children of their own, and he would smile at them the same way. She took his arm, and they resumed their walk.

It should have been peaceful. It might have been, were Ciro not such a stubborn man.

"I'm only concerned about your well-being, *mi amor*." Ciro squeezed her hand, continuing the conversation they'd let lapse.

She rolled her eyes. It was always the same line with him. "I'm fine here, among my people." It was true enough, Ayelen thought. She'd spent so much of her childhood with the Spanish colonists, trying to fit in with the society her father had come from, but had never felt at home there like she did among the Wayuu, her mother's people. "Really, I've never been happier."

Matias, her brother, choked back a laugh from behind them. "That's not much to go by. You were as miserable living among the Spaniards as I was."

Involuntarily, Ayelen held herself taller, wrapping the simple dress of her people closer around her body. "Those Spanish girls were small-minded, that's all."

Ciro stopped and turned to her. The gentle breeze from the nearby foothills passed between them, bringing with it the scents and sounds of the not-too-distant jungle. "You're not happy here. I see it in your eyes and in the way you smile. Let's leave all this behind. Sail with me to Spain, and we'll start over. No one there will expect you to be anything more than what you choose to be."

Fire filled Ayelen's soul as she looked at her husband's kind, blue eyes. "I *choose* to be here with my people. I'm of the Zyanya family. It is my duty to stay here and protect my people."

Ciro sighed and pulled her close. The warm solidity of his body and the strength of his arms around her never failed to break through to her. She allowed herself to relax against him.

"Even though they don't see you?" he said gently. "They want you to be something else, and you're tearing yourself apart trying to be what they want you to be."

Ayelen leaned against him as he stroked her hair, her arms held loosely around his waist. Yes, they expected much of her. Especially now that she had begun learning Dream Talking — the hereditary ability to move through, and communicate with, the spirit world. Things the Old One and her mother had told her as simple stories in her youth were so much more burdensome now that they were real. Not even Dream Talking was what she'd expected it to be. But she did want them. She wanted to fit in with her people, the Wayuu, more than anything.

"Besides," Ciro continued when she didn't respond, "once you're free of all this pressure …."

Ayelen immediately tensed, and Ciro trailed off. She knew what he was thinking: that their inability to conceive was because of her stress. It would be the start of the same painful discussion they'd had a hundred times before. With a sigh, he dropped his hands away from her before she could jerk herself free. They'd only known each other for three years, and he knew her so well. And yet, sometimes it still felt like he didn't know her at all.

"How many times are we going to go over this?" She shook her head at him. Why couldn't he understand? "I'm not giving up my place here, regardless of what you think about it—"

"And if the Old One says she'll have a daughter," Matias cut in, parroting back the words Ayelen had said too many times, "then she'll have a daughter."

"Someday." Ciro waved his hand and turned away, frustrated. "I know, I know."

Ayelen stayed where she was, her arms folded defensively across her chest. Why couldn't he understand that she wanted children, too? That it tore at her heart that they'd been married nearly two years already, and still she remained barren?

Ciro turned back to her, pinching the bridge of his nose. "I want to believe in your people's superstitions, I really do. But how can she *know*?"

Because she saw it in the Dream. The words were on the tip of her tongue. *Because* I've *seen it in the Dream.* But she couldn't. No matter how much she loved him, or he her, he wouldn't believe it. He loved his religion and the science that filled his ships' sails and had carried him across the world. He didn't have room in his worldview for things of the spirit. Instead, she closed her mouth and glared at him.

Ciro growled and turned away.

"There, there, now, children," Matias piped up with his best imitation of the arrogant *duenna* they'd had as children, stepping between Ayelen and her husband. "No more talking from either of you until you can say something nice, or else you'll get no fruit with your supper."

Ciro groaned. Ayelen glared at Matias, but her twin brother just arched his eyebrow. He mirrored her expression, unblinking, until she cracked a smile and turned away. Matias linked his right arm in hers and led her over to Ciro, taking him with his left.

Ayelen rolled her eyes as her brother led them further along the path. The sun had set fully, and the stars began to appear in the moonless night sky.

"I'm sorry, *mi amor*," Ciro said after a minute, looking across his brother-in-law to his wife.

"Oh, Ciro." Matias fanned himself with his hand and leaned up against Ciro. "I'm so flattered. Whatever will your wife say, though?"

"Get lost." Ciro shoved Matias playfully away.

Matias stumbled, dragging his sister back with him. "Where I go, she goes! You don't get one without the other!"

"I rue the day I first saw your ugly face." Ciro laughed, lunging after Matias. He knocked him to his knees as Ayelen broke free of them both. "And I curse the horse you rode in on for all the trouble you put me through."

Matias half-turned and kicked at Ciro, his boot connecting solidly with his friend's shoulder. The kick knocked Ciro back, and Matias scrambled back to his feet. "Except that you'd have never met my sister if you weren't half in love with my ugly face from the beginning."

Ayelen watched, exasperated, her arms folded across her chest. "Get up out of the dirt, the both of you. I'm not going to be washing your shirts myself if you stain them."

Matias immediately dropped to his knees before her and bowed. "Oh, forgive me, great and mighty Zyanya! May the Old One curse our house to ever have daughters first-born."

"Get up, you fool." Ayelen grabbed his elbow and pulled her brother to his feet.

"Oh, wait, that's already been done," Matias said, casting Ciro a thoughtful look. "What other curse should I have for disrespecting my older sister?"

Ciro sidled up to Ayelen. "I could hold him down for you …"

Ayelen nodded thoughtfully. "While I let all the village children tickle his feet with feathers."

"Nooo!" Matias grabbed his sister's hands. "Not feathers! Anything but that!"

"Well, I suppose I could forgo the feathers." Ayelen looked from her brother to her husband, a contentedness filling her. "But you're still washing your own clothes for this."

Ciro met her gaze and pulled her close, and for a moment, the world around them fell away. The starlight cast a pale illumination over the quiet landscape as she turned her face toward his.

A scream rent the silence of the night, and they jerked apart, Ayelen's heart leaping into her throat. Ciro moved her behind him protectively, turning toward the sound.

Another heartrending scream tore through the night, followed by distant shouts of men from the village. Ciro backed them away from the path and into the grass. A shadow moved toward them from the direction of the village. It resolved into the form of a hunched, man-like creature, leaping across the grasses as it ran.

Its gait seemed strained, as though unable to decide if it would run faster on foot like a man, or on all fours, like a large cat. Before Ayelen could catch her breath, the shadowy creature reached them. Its long tail of darkness whipped past, leaving in its wake a foul stench of both putrescence and evil. Whatever it was, Ayelen knew she couldn't let it escape to attack someone else. Yanking her arm from Ciro's grip, she ran after it.

2

CIRO CURSED at the lithe form of his wife sprinting away. He hesitated a moment, turning back to Matias, who had dropped into a crouch, his head hidden in his arms. He didn't have time for this. He yanked his brother-in-law to his feet.

He shoved Matias toward the village. "Find whoever that thing hurt and help them. I'm going after your fool sister," he growled, breaking into a sprint after his wife. *Someone's got to stop her from getting herself killed.*

The grass crackled beneath his boots. What was she thinking? She didn't even have any weapons on her. Except maybe a knife, for whatever use that would be. He ran through grassy field, dodging between the scrubby trees that dotted the landscape, hoping he wouldn't trip over a rock and break his ankle in the starlit darkness.

He closed in on Ayelen, something he hadn't actually thought he could do. Realization that she had slowed stung his pride as she came to a stop. "Thank providence," he muttered, coming to a stop beside her.

He scanned the tree line in the distance for movement. "Is it gone, then? Are you all right?"

"It outran me." Bitterness colored her voice.

"What do you think you were doing?" Ciro's fear pressed against his throat as he stepped close to her. "What if it had turned on you? What if you'd been hurt?" His voice cracked. "What if you'd been killed?"

She waved away his concern, turning back to the village, her flowing, patterned dress a colorless flutter as she moved. "Well, it didn't, and I wasn't. It's fine."

He followed, brooding. Her reassurances were anything but. It had been one thing for Ciro to risk his own life out here in the wilderness of the Wayuu territory, but keeping his family here was entirely something else. Ayelen had lived half her life among Spanish colonialists, her father's people. No matter what she thought, she didn't belong out here. It wasn't safe.

She slipped her hand into his. Its warm petiteness brought his mind back to her as she spoke. "Besides, I'm here, and I can help."

"How?" he said, failing to keep the stinging sarcasm entirely at bay.

She bristled. "Do you have any idea what that thing was? Because I do." Ayelen paused and looked up at the stars.

He came to a halt beside her, watching her face.

"Kanaima. Do you even know that word, *mi amor?*"

Ciro racked his brain. Up until three years ago, he'd only spoken a smattering of Wayuunaiki. Proficient as he was now, he still didn't know the term.

"It's a demon spirit, bound within the body of a man, usually a warrior."

Of course it is. Ciro withheld his disbelief, reminding himself that what mattered was that *she* believed it.

"Not just any warrior, though. One who has suffered great loss and sworn vengeance upon his enemies. To exact his revenge, he binds himself to a powerful spirit to give him power." She pulled her long, dark braid over her shoulder. "However, once he has begun this journey, he cannot stop until he has completed his task. The longer he stays bonded with the demon spirit, the more corrupt he becomes, until he is little more than a monster, roaming the land and killing whatever he finds. Except for infants, oddly enough. They say a kanaima can't see babies, which seems strange to me."

"And what exactly makes you so especially qualified to manage it? Sounds like he needs an exorcism."

Ayelen actually laughed. "You could call it that. What's needed is a Dream Talker, someone who can free the man's spirit from the hold of the demon's."

"Which the Old One supposedly is, and you are not yet. So there's no need for you to go after it." He took her hands and met her eyes. "Send a messenger to her, and don't get involved."

"You don't understand. If he came here and attacked someone once, he'll do it again. The village will not be safe until that thing is destroyed. I am of the Zyanya family line. I am a Dream Talker, and I must protect my people."

And we're back to that. Ciro sighed and dropped the subject, and they began toward the village. He'd need to find a different way to convince her. Perhaps her brother could help.

3

CIRO DUCKED THROUGH the doorway of his family's small home, his mind abuzz with things he could have said to change Ayelen's mind. The loosely woven wood-and-mud walls below the thatched roof kept the small building shaded and private, while allowing airflow. Though the air here wasn't nearly as muggy as the Caribbean waterfront he had traveled from, it could still become unbearable. Abrupt movement from the hammock in the corner told him Matias had returned but had not yet fallen asleep.

"Are you all right, brother?" he asked, setting his candle down on the small table. Matias only shifted in his hammock, turning to face the wall. "Have you heard any news on who was attacked?"

Ciro allowed the silence, waiting for his friend to respond. He dearly hoped it wasn't little Muusa or her sister, but the villagers were tight-lipped with him sometimes. *Alijuna* — outsider — that he was, they hadn't said. Waiting for Matias to speak, he washed the dirt and sweat from his face. The sounds of Ayelen gathering her gear to go after the monster floated through the walls into the dimly lit room.

"Ayelen insists on going after the thing. She called it kanaima, whatever that is." Ciro waited a moment, hoping Matias would respond. "Whatever it is, she is no match for it and needs to be stopped."

When Matias again failed to respond, Ciro had had enough. He stepped up to his brother-in-law's hammock and pushed it. Matias looked up at him. The younger man met Ciro's gaze for a moment.

Wetness in Matias's dark eyes glinted in the flickering candlelight for a moment before he looked away. "No," he said, his voice thick with emotion. "If I were interested in domestic strife, I'd have married some lovely *señorita* with shiny hair already. Leave me out of it."

Ciro poked his friend's side, holding back his frustration. "This isn't about my marriage; it's about your sister. Aren't you at all upset that she plans to hunt down some demon, will likely get hurt if not killed, and you plan to just lie here and do nothing?"

Matias curled in on himself, turning away again to stare at the wall. "No."

"This is why the Good Lord never gave me siblings," Ciro muttered to himself. Bracing himself, he grabbing the hammock and dumped Matias on the ground.

"Get up and help me talk sense into your sister." Ciro held his hand out to help Matias. Matias looked ruefully at it for a moment before reaching up. Ciro pulled him to a stand, but he could tell Matias's heart wasn't in it as he guided him out the door.

Outside, Ayelen had gathered a small pile of gear; foodstuffs for a couple days, a rolled blanket, and a knife. Ciro hefted the pack and pushed it into Matias's arms. "Go put this away."

"Don't you dare!" Ayelen hissed, coming around the corner of the building, the light of the newly risen moon glinting across her black hair. Matias held the pack to his chest and tried to disappear against the wall as his sister stalked up to Ciro.

"We agreed to wait for the village elders to return," Ciro said, stepping into her path.

"I made no such agreement." Ayelen tried to side step him, but he moved again to block her.

"You've got to see reason, Ayelen. You can't just go charging off in the middle of the night." Ciro ran his hands through his hair. "You don't even know the first thing about fighting. How are you going to stop a crazy warrior, possessed or not? He'll gut you the moment he sees you."

"Who says he has to see me?" She crossed her arms over her chest, all the stubbornness and fire that had first attracted him to her blazing in her eyes.

He scowled. She was absolutely infuriating. "If you don't need to get close to him, why can't you just do your Dream Talking thing from the safety of your own bed?"

"I have to at least be nearby so I can sever the ties between the man's spirit and the demon's."

"And what if he sees you and attacks? How will you defend yourself if you're busy being unconscious?"

"That won't happen." She turned from him.

Her refusal to accept the possibility of danger beyond her immediate concern made Ciro want to break something. Instead, he put his hand on the doorframe and gripped it, squeezing until his fingers hurt. With a deep breath, he let his anger flow from his body as he exhaled. Taking her elbow, he let his fingers trail down her arm to her hand. "Why not wait? There are guards on watch against another attack tonight. Everyone here is safe for now. I know you feel like you need to prove something to these people, but you can't do that if you get yourself killed."

Ayelen closed her eyes. He tried pulling her toward him, hopeful that he'd gotten through to her. Instead, she jerked her arm from his grasp and glared at him, tears glistening in her eyes.

"I can't believe you," she said, her low voice thick with emotion. "You're just like every last one of *them*. Those arrogant *señoritas* thought I couldn't be more than an imbecile because of my mother's blood. My mother's people wait with their silent, judgmental eyes to see if I'm more Wayuu or *alijuna*. You, my husband, are supposed to be supporting me. But for all your words of love and confidence, at the first chance I have to prove myself, you insist on holding me back.

"And *you!*" Ayelen turned her fury toward her brother, who shrank back further. "You're supporting him! I don't know what's changed in you so much the last few years, but I never expected you to turn against me too. We're *family*! I thought that meant something to you!"

"Ayelen!" Ciro cut her off, stepping between the siblings, shocked to hear her yell at her brother.

"Don't bother, Ciro," Matias said from behind him, the bitterness in his voice cutting. "A spitting cat with its own tail in its teeth never bit anybody."

Ayelen rocked back as though she'd been slapped. "Get out of my home," she hissed.

Matias tossed the gear he'd been holding at her feet and walked away in heavy silence.

4

SOMEHOW, IN THE darkness, their small home felt exceptionally empty. Ciro's warm arms wrapped around her on the hammock as he snored gently. Ayelen hadn't actually expected her brother to leave. She hadn't wanted him to, not really. But he had anyway. He was her other half. He'd always been there for her, and watching him walk away had felt like tearing her soul in two.

The shock of her brother's action had stopped further argument with her husband and she'd numbly agreed to wait for news from the elders. She drifted in and out of sleep in the late night. The sounds of the gentle wind and songs of the crickets wove through her mind while the world swayed softly beneath her hammock.

In her mind, she stood out in the field in the grass, as she had earlier that evening. Her half-conscious mind felt Ciro stir in his sleep, and she set her hand on his chest to soothe him. He stilled, and Ayelen opened her mind more fully to the Dream.

The stars shone down, brilliant through the deep blue sky. The wind pulled playfully at her hair like a pesky dog, full of the scent of rain, and she batted it away. It pushed her forward, and she turned away from its grasp. Across the field lay the barren, arid desert of the northern land. In the far distance a woman with long, silver hair watched. *Nana!* Ayelen smiled and waved to the Old One. The woman nodded back, gesturing for Ayelen to look behind her.

Ayelen turned back toward the jungle-covered mountain beyond the foothills, and a stench passed her, turning her stomach; vile, putrid, and dark. Twisted. The wind again pushed her forward.

But Ciro... The thought escaped her before she could stop it, and she turned back toward her village. Lining the path lay the bodies of the villagers, their faces each covered with a square of white cloth. At the foremost lay her husband and her brother.

Determination warred with fear in her chest as she turned back to the jungle. A calm certainty descended over her, stilling her pounding heart and unsettled stomach, despite the trail of vile, black smoke. Squaring her shoulders, she took a step forward.

And woke.

Ayelen lay in the darkness of her small home, still in her husband's warm arms. His chest rose and fell beneath her hand, his heartbeat clear and calm. Her own heartbeat raced, her muscles tense. The Dream had been clear.

If she didn't go, everyone would die.

The fear that had gripped her heart at the sight of Ciro and Matias dead returned. She could not take them along. She couldn't bear to have them hurt.

As quietly as she could, she slipped from the hammock and dressed. At the door, she gave one quick look back to her sleeping husband, her heart full of love for him. "I'll see you soon, *mi amor,*" she whispered, and slipped into the dark night.

5

CIRO STARTED AWAKE, momentarily unsure of where he was in the dark, gently swinging hammock. The silence stretched across the dark night, signaling the earliest of hours when no sane thing remained awake. The wood and woven walls of his Wayuu home resolved themselves in the pale moonlight, and the world righted itself in his mind. He shifted, his left arm pulling toward him. Empty.

With his heart in his throat, he bolted out of bed. *Please let her be nearby!*

"Ayelen!" He called out to her quietly. Perhaps she had merely been restless. As much as he wanted to believe it, the sinking feeling in his gut only became worse as he lit the candle. He pushed open the door and out to the shaded awning. Her pack was gone.

He ran through the village toward the hills, pausing to peer between the buildings he passed. Perhaps he'd only just missed her.

The buildings gave way to the open field, the jungle just beyond. The moonlight in the clear summer sky showed him the empty, silvery field, the grasses dancing in the gentle breeze.

Cursing the self-destructive foolishness of headstrong women, Ciro ran back to their home and threw together a travelling pack. Had she really needed to leave in the middle of the night? How much of a head start did she have?

He shoved a change of clothes viciously into the bag. If she had gone on horseback, she'd have a serious lead on him. And he only assumed she'd headed toward the jungle. He ducked into the house, pulling out his cutlass from beneath a pile of blankets. Had she had the foresight to at least take a knife? Though he hated to admit it, Ciro was a sailor and a merchant, not a woodsman. He would need help tracking her down. He needed Matias.

Striding across the way to the open central awning, Ciro strapped on his sword. Several hammocks hung there, each filled with a sleeping occupant. Matias's hammock was easy to make out in the darkness with its distinctive white and red pattern. Ayelen had made it for her brother when she'd first learned to weave. Their own hammock had a matching pattern.

He gently shook his brother-in-law's hammock. "Matias!" he hissed, trying to wake him without waking the others.

"It's too early to milk goats," Matias muttered, swatting at Ciro. Despite everything, it made him smile. He wished he could have responded with a quip, but he didn't have the time.

"Ayelen is missing," he said quietly.

"And this is new, how?" Matias opened one sleepy eye.

"I don't have time for your jokes this morning, *waré*. I need to bring her back before she gets killed."

Matias sat up in his hammock. "I don't see what that has to do with me. She made it very clear that she doesn't want me in her life."

"You can wallow in your self-pity later. Right now I need you to help me find my wife. I have no idea how to track, and you're the best tracker I've ever seen. If you don't help me, it won't just be your sister you'll be burying, but your brother-in-law and best friend as well."

"Fine." Matias grudgingly got out of his hammock. "But we're only finding her and bringing her back. Nothing more."

"Nothing more. Now let's go."

6

THE HORSES' HOOVES hit the jungle floor with muted thuds. Matias rode ahead of Ciro, his shoulders rounded and his coat tight as though to protect him from some unseen force. The sunrise filtered through the thick canopy, casting shadows over his friend's coat, while the birds began their morning calls.

Ciro watched him as they moved beneath the patchwork of shadows. Did it have something to do with how upset he'd been after the kanaima's attack, or was he just unhappy to be out here? They'd ridden in silence for hours, Matias leading them forward without hesitation. The man had such spirit the first time Ciro had met him. He'd been just as fiery as his twin sister, full of laughter and joy, but somewhere along the line, Matias's spark had begun to dim.

Ciro thought back. Had it been losing his sister to marriage, perhaps? Ciro shook his head. Matias had been ecstatic to see the two of them together. He'd helped Ciro learn the Wayuu's dances in order to court Ayelen properly. He'd even stolen Ayelen's prized jewel — a stone of *tu'uma* — for him to put in a setting in an attempt to impress her. What Matias had neglected to tell him was that the stone was also a precious family heirloom, handed down from mother to daughter for generations, and purportedly gifted to the first Zyanya by the family spirit guide. Ciro smiled, his hands resting lightly across the saddle. Ayelen had broken things off with him for that, and it had been Matias who had smoothed them over again.

No, the changes had started even before then. He'd been haunted since they'd left Maracaibo together, though he tried to hide it behind smiles and laughter. Ciro had been too occupied by his own life to notice the change in his friend at the time. Or since. Shame pricked his consciousness, and he kicked his horse forward to ride beside Matias.

"I've been thinking," Ciro said, pausing for the quip from Matias about his intelligence. When it didn't come, he continued. "I can hardly believe it's been — what? Three years since I followed you out of Maracaibo. Four?"

Matias shrugged and kept his gaze sullenly ahead of him.

"Anyhow, a lot has changed since then, right? I was a young merchant, and the world was my oyster, really. You were what, eighteen?"

Matias shrugged again, and Ciro rolled his eyes.

"What's wrong?"

Again Ciro was treated to silence.

"I've never heard you go so much as two minutes without talking, and no longer than an hour without some joke. You haven't even smiled since yesterday."

Matias turned to him and bared his teeth in an aggressive approximation of a smile. "Better?"

"Really?"

"What?" Matias jerked his hand into the air, startling Ciro's horse. "You wake me up in the middle of the night to tell me to ride with you to prevent my sister's certain death. Do you expect that I should go to it singing songs of joy and glory?"

"I didn't say that—"

"Look, just because Ayelen is all torn up inside about where she belongs and what she is doesn't mean I am, too. Life here is simple: protect my family, live with honor, contribute to the welfare of the village and the people. It's all I'm trying to do; I don't know why you two can't just let me have that."

As much as Ciro wanted to point out that bringing his sister home fulfilled all three of those tenets, the bitterness in Matias's voice stopped him. Ciro wanted to push Matias to explain what was bothering him, but nothing useful would be gained by fighting between themselves.

Perhaps a different tack would help. "Did I ever tell you why I left Maracaibo?"

Matias grunted.

"I've always felt it was Providence that kept us running into each other. I'd done some business with your father, of course. He ran my goods along the trading lines to the north and west. I had a booming business there, built from hard work, both mine and the people I worked with. You and your father were some of the best."

Ciro glanced at Matias, hoping the mention of his recently deceased father would give away something. Matias's face remained stoic, so Ciro continued.

"I did, however, make some poor choices in partners." Ciro leaned back in his saddle, stretching his stiff back. "Antonio Gonza. Now that was a mixed blessing if ever one existed. We got our start together; we helped each other become more successful than either of us had imagined possible. For five years, we were practically inseparable, always there for each other. But then ..." Ciro shrugged and waited.

Matias simply shifted in his own saddle.

Ciro sighed. "Then we had a disagreement over ethics, so I bought his shares of the company, and we parted ways. Amicably, I thought. Unfortunately one thing led to another, and he got into some trouble. Long story short, he felt that it would be best to have me killed. So, instead of facing him down, I ran away."

Matias looked over, skepticism written across his face.

Ciro hid a smile. He'd gotten his friend to respond. "Indeed. I, Ciro Alvarez Bosque, ran from that fight. I knew I couldn't win it; he had half the underbelly of the Maracaibo hunting me, offering quite the ransom for my head. So, one night, I quietly set my affairs in trusted hands, and snuck off with a caravan to the

North, led by someone I knew I could trust: your father."

"And you never went back." Matias said, his voice flat.

"And I never went back." Ciro nodded. "Perhaps I should have, just to settle things with Gonza. But now I have a family to care for, a family that I love and who mean the world to me, and I'd do anything to keep them safe."

"That's why you've been pressuring her to go to Spain with you, isn't it?"

Ciro nodded. "I should have told you both sooner that I'm a hunted man, but there's no reason anyone should know I'm here. If they haven't found me by now, they're not going to."

They lapsed into silence as Matias guided them unerringly through the trees.

"The thing I've learned about being hunted is that you can't just stop living because of fear. The world keeps spinning, and if you don't join in the dance of it, life will leave you behind." He smiled, recalling his first sight of Ayelen, spinning to the beat of a tribal dance by the firelight. He'd had the chance that night to join, but he had declined and had watched her dance away from him with his heart. "Your sister taught me that."

"Is that why you fight with her so much?"

The question made Ciro pause. They didn't fight all that much, did they? He reflected over the last several days. Yes, they had argued several times, but he didn't consider it fighting. "She's just stubborn," he said finally. "If she'd just listen to me, I know she'd see it my way, but she's so convinced she's right that she won't take a moment to consider anyone else's viewpoint."

"Said the pot of the kettle."

"I think you mean it the other way round. I have nothing on her, when she digs her heels in."

"Did you know," Matias said, setting his voice to the same timbre the Wayuu storytellers used, "that you can teach a colt to fall over on command?"

"And what has that to do with the trade winds of India?" Ciro asked.

"It's very simple, actually. You need only put the halter on a young colt and pull. The colt will resist the forward force on his head by leaning back, matching force for force, until he falls over."

"That's because horses are stupid." Ciro gave a friendly pat on his own horse's neck. "It should just walk forward."

Matias continued, undisturbed by Ciro's commentary. "Do it enough times, and as soon as you so much as touch the lead rope, the colt will simply fall over. It's a wonderful trick. But you must be careful to do it right. If you're foolish enough to stand beside the colt and gently walk forward with it, it might step forward, too. And soon, instead of falling over, why, the colt would be walking with you, willingly following your lead." Matias turned in his saddle to look squarely at Ciro. "And what a shame that would be."

Ciro grabbed a handful of leaves from a nearby tree and threw them at his friend. What did Matias know about relationships, anyway?

7

THE AFTERNOON SUNLIGHT filtered through the thick canopy, casting slanted beams across the dancing pollen. The muggy air filled Ayelen's lungs and chest with its heaviness and the foul trail of her quarry. The silence among the foliage told her she was getting closer. Perhaps she would catch up with the creature that evening and return home before sunrise.

She pulled her horse to a stop and dismounted, ready for a break from the saddle. She needed to plan her approach beyond simply cutting free the man's soul from that of the demon's. Images of the way the villagers would cheer her as she rode triumphantly back into the village filled her mind. They would encircle her, proud to call her their own. The elders would return and give her approving smiles. Ciro would be the proudest, sweeping her off her feet at his joy at her safe return. When she told him of her triumph, he would finally understand …

A noise in the underbrush startled her, and she spun putting the horse to her back and pulling the knife from her belt. Ciro thought her incapable of defending herself, but what did he know, soft city merchant that he was? A small smile tugged at her lips at the absurdity of calling her well-muscled husband soft.

A gentle rustling of the underbrush, clearly from a large animal, came closer. Too noisy for a deer or predator. Someone had followed her. She maneuvered her horse behind one of the tall tree roots and moved to the other side of the small path, crouching in the underbrush. A minute passed and the animal came closer, still hidden by the large trees. Another minute. Couldn't whoever it was ride faster? Her thighs began to ache, and she rubbed them with one hand, the other holding the knife before her.

Finally, the rider came into view, and she growled. Ciro had followed her. Impossible man. Ciro's horse neighed a greeting to its herd-mate, and her horse returned the greeting. The traitor.

Ciro pulled up alongside her sociable horse and looked around. "Where's your rider, hey?"

Ha, he didn't see her. She backed farther into the underbrush. She'd just wait until he started looking for her, get back onto her own horse, and then sneak off. He was no tracker, he'd never be able to follow her—

A hand snaked around her head, covering her mouth, and another took hold of her knife hand. A moment of panic froze her to the spot before she began to struggle violently. She could cry out, but then Ciro would help and he'd be even more certain she couldn't take care of herself. Instead, she flung her head backwards, hoping to head-butt her assailant's nose, and threw her weight back to throw them both off balance. Instead, her head hit nothing, and the body behind hers met with an equal force pushing forwards.

"Sorry, you've tried that one on me too many times to fall for it again." Her brother's voice beside her ear sent a wave of relief through her, and she batted at his face with her free hand as he let her go.

"What are you doing here?"

"We came for you," Ciro said, standing before her.

"Bah!" She waved them both away and stood, brushing off the ground debris from her dress. "I don't need your help. Go away."

Ciro took her hand, and she allowed him to lead her back to the horses.

"I'm going to get my horse," Matias announced, following the path Ciro had come down. The moment he was out of sight, Ciro pulled her into his arms, crushing her to him and kissed her. For a moment, she allowed herself to be lost in his embrace, the familiar comfort of his strength, and the smell of cloves and wood smoke. They broke apart, and she lay her head on his shoulder, not ready for the moment of peace between them to end. But it would. He would insist that she give up, and she couldn't.

He drew in a breath to speak, and she set her fingers to his lips.

"Don't." She looked up at him. "Nothing you can say will make me turn back, and I don't want to fight you."

Gently, he covered her hand with his and pulled it away from his face. "We've all had a long day, and the horses need a rest. Perhaps we'll all think more clearly once we've had something to eat."

She bristled at the implication that she was being irrational, as if food would change her mind. A cutting retort sat on the tip of her tongue. But hadn't she just said she didn't want to fight? She closed her mouth and swallowed it back. Maybe *she'd* be able to convince *him* once he'd had something to eat. Instead of arguing, she smiled. "Agreed."

8

THEY BUILT A small fire, and Ayelen sat beside it cooking a small gourd of porridge, with a leaf covered with berries from Matias beside her. Ciro brushed down the horses, picketed several feet away, cleaning off the dried sweat and dirt that clung to their coats marking the edges of where the saddles had sat. Ayelen's horse reached back and nipped at him as he brushed over its sensitive flank.

"I know, *muchacho*." Ciro rubbed the horse's nose. "It's been a long day, but with any luck, you'll be home by morning and getting fat and lazy on the grass."

"I wouldn't count on it," Matias came around the other side of the horse and patted it on the back.

"You don't think I can convince her to go back?" Ciro lowered his voice, moving on to his own horse while Matias began on the third.

"I love you like a brother, Ciro, but some days you're as dense as a stone dropped off a cliff."

"Maybe if you'd work on saying what you mean rather than squeaking like an old bat."

"Only a fool tries to get between a hound and its prey." Matias leaned against his horse, tossing the brush into the air with a spin and catching it.

"Are you calling my wife a dog?"

"No, I'm calling you an idiot." He tossed the brush to Ciro.

"Good. Otherwise, I might have to defend her honor, and I'm far too tired for that today." Ciro set the brush in the open saddlebag.

Matias leaned across Ciro's horse. "You know as well as I do that even if you get her to go back with us, she'll just sneak off again."

"So I'll tie her to her horse."

Matias raised an eyebrow at him. "Because dragging the colt forward has worked so well for you so far."

9

AYELEN STIRRED THE porridge as it boiled, listening to the men speaking quietly beside the horses. She loved the deep sound of her husband's voice and his Spanish accent on her native language. Her brother's lighter tenor floated above it. He had always worked hard to make sure that no trace of the *alijuna* accent came through in his Wayuunaiki. Though their company was nice, she needed them to go back. What if they got hurt?

The kanaima was near. Its rancid odor surrounded her whenever the wind slowed. Then the breeze would move again and clear the scent. If she kept going, surely she could find where it rested tonight, and free the man from the cat-demon. Ciro seemed to think it would be dangerous, but so long as the thing slept, what harm could there be?

Ciro sat down beside her, dropping more firewood onto the small pile while Matias took the spoon from her and ladled the sticky porridge into bowls.

"I think it would be best for us to rest here for the evening and head back tomorrow." Ciro took a bowl from Matias.

Ayelen crossed her arms across her chest and glared at him. Matias shoved her bowl at her. Relenting, she accepted it with a nod of gratitude to her brother. "Thank you, but I'm not leaving without finding the kanaima. Nothing you can say will change that."

Matias sat back and gave Ciro a wide-eyed look, as though their exchange was a fascinating sport. She watched emotions cross her husband's face at her refusal. She could be every bit as stubborn as him.

"We are staying with you, one way or the other."

Matias turned his over-acted gaze back to his sister.

"You're not going to stop me from finding the kanaima."

Matias turned back to Ciro, resting his chin on his hands.

"No one will go anywhere tonight. And if we find it—"

"When."

"—*If* we find it, we will mark its lair and return to the village for reinforcements."

Ayelen slammed her bowl onto the trunk she sat on. "That's not—!"

"We're not prepared to fight anything here! Matias and I together might, *might*, be able to take down a trained soldier. We're not fighters, Ayelen. We don't have the skill or the experience for this without serious risk of one or both of us getting hurt, possibly even killed. Is that really a risk you want to take?"

Ayelen leaned back, pressing her lips together. But her words wouldn't stay put. "You're right; you have no business being here. That's why I left without you. I didn't ask you to come. I didn't want you here."

"Well, this has been lovely," Matias cut in when Ayelen drew breath to continue, "but I'm rather done for the night. Let's turn in, shall we?"

Without waiting for further comment, her brother moved to the hammock he'd hung in a nearby tree and lay down, his back to the fire, wrapping himself in his thin blanket.

"Ayelen," Ciro said, exasperated.

"Stop talking. I want to sleep," Matias announced. "And I don't want any horses falling on me."

"What?" Ayelen mouthed silently to Ciro, gesturing to her crazy twin.

Ciro rolled his eyes and moved to sit beside her, his back to the fire. "He thinks I'm an idiot," he said quietly.

"That's because you are," Matias said from his blankets. "No more talking."

Ciro pushed her hair away from her ear and moved close, whispering to her. His nearness never failed to send a thrill through her body. "Can we at least agree that you won't fight the thing if we find it? If it attacks, let me protect you?"

She lay her arm around his waist and whispered back, her lips nearly brushing his ear. "If you agree to take Matias and go back so I can free the man from the kanaima's control, I promise not to confront it."

He pulled her onto his lap, and she wrapped her arms around his shoulders. "I could never let you go alone into danger. If you agree not to leave without me again, and to not confront this demon, I will not get in the way of your Dream Talking mission of healing."

"I can hear you two whispering," Matias mumbled.

"Are you sure we can't tie him to his horse and send him back?" Ayelen asked, just loud enough for Matias to make out.

"That's it. I'm sleeping by the horses." Matias gathered his bedding and stalked off. They watched him go until Ayelen turned Ciro's head back to hers.

"It's a deal," she said, and kissed his jaw.

10

THE GREY, PRE-DAWN light cast an even, dull glow across the jungle when Ayelen awoke. Despite her desire to stay beside her husband's warm bulk, she needed to get up. As she reached to untuck the blanket that had protected them from the pesky insects, Ciro stirred and pulled her back beside him.

"I'm not going anywhere, *mi amor*," she whispered, kissing his cheek. He grumbled and shifted, and she stood from the hammock. After slipping on her sandals, she ducked out from the canvas they'd put up to keep off the rain, and stretched. The fresh layer of mud on the jungle floor sucked gently at her shoes while she walked, and she sent a prayer of gratitude to her forefathers that it hadn't rained harder.

After relieving herself, she made her way to check on the horses. Her horse nickered as she neared.

"You hungry this morning?" she asked, pulling his grain bag from the saddle bag. Her horse snorted and backed away. Now that was strange. "Come here, you silly thing, I have food for you."

The horse backed away further, into the other two, who were equally agitated. Ciro's horse reared, his eyes wide, and the sudden stench of decay nearly knocked her down. She spun and came face-to-face with the demon.

He stood within arm's reach of her, half-crouched, with a long, curved black knife in one hand. For a moment, she stood frozen, her eyes travelling from the wicked-looking knife up his lean, muscled arms with their mottled, dirty skin. He wore a dark, filthy loincloth and black jaguar skin across his shoulders, its head over his brow. Around his neck lay a necklace of sacred *tu'uma* and long dark claws. How dare he create such an abomination? A fire flickered to life inside her. His wild black hair in carib braids framed a face marred by scars that flowed and curled beneath his eyes like a jaguar's marks.

Reaching for her knife, she met his eyes. The eyes, glazed over in white, looked right at her, and her vision went double, the man overlaid with the jaguar's soul. It snarled and fought against the invisible binding that held it fast as the kanaima channeled the jaguar's anger and pain into its lust for blood. The wrongness of it sickened her. Behind her, the horses again called out, and the kanaima cocked its head and sniffed.

To her right, the sound of Ciro knocking his boots together to dislodge visitors from them sounded like gunshots to her heart. She and the kanaima both turned to the sound, fear twisting her stomach. The kanaima shot forward.

"Ciro!" Ayelen screamed, but as she turned to follow it, something knocked her to the ground.

"Don't you dare," hissed her brother as they landed in the mud. "It'll kill you."

She struggled against him, elbowing him in the chest. She clawed at his hands, listening desperately for Ciro. Had he kept his cutlass nearby? There was a snarl and a thud, and Ayelen strained her head to see what was happening.

"Let me go," she hissed, kicking her brother's thigh. He grunted and loosened his grip for a moment, enough for her to turn and see Ciro staggering back to his feet, his sword before him. The thing jumped at Ciro, and Ayelen twisted, throwing all her weight into swinging her elbow at her brother's gut. He gasped and let her go. Desperately, she crawled forward, pulling herself to her feet.

The kanaima knocked Ciro to the ground. They had both lost their blades, and they grappled in the mud. Ayelen ran forward, pausing to scoop up the kanaima's dark, curved blade. The kanaima landed atop Ciro, pinning him. It raised its hand, the fingers like long, black claws and swiped down at Ciro, even as Ayelen leapt forward, plunging the knife into its back.

As it landed its blow across Ciro's chest and arm, the kanaima screamed, and spun, knocking Ayelen back. She lost her grip on the knife but kept her feet while the thing searched for what had attacked it. Its eyes swept past Ayelen, though she stood but two steps away. It screamed again and darted off, running back into the jungle.

The thought to follow it didn't even cross her mind as Ayelen dropped to her knees next to Ciro.

"Please don't die," she repeated under her breath cutting away the torn shirt. Beside her, Matias stood and handed her a canteen of water. She ripped the shirt into strips and wadded them against the bleeding wounds. Ciro grunted and trembled, and Matias turned away to retch.

"Pull yourself together, Matias. I need you." She pulled the cloth away to pour the water across her husband's chest. Ciro moaned softly and tried to push her away. She knocked his hand away. Ants nearly half the length of her finger began to crawl onto his skin. Her heartbeat pounded in her ears as she brushed the ants away, praying she could get them all before they began to sting. She moved to his head, trying to sit him up. "Matias! You've got to help me get him off the ground. The ants!"

Shakily, Matias stood beside her, and together they got Ciro to a stand. The insects swarmed to the pool of blood he left behind. Frantically, she batted at his clothes, knocking away the things that still crawled on Ciro as they helped him to the hammock. His breath came heavily, and with a shuddering sigh of relief, he relaxed across the hammock, his feet dangling a handsbreadth from the ground.

"Bring me the *chirrinchi* and a clean shirt, and get the fire going," Ayelen instructed Matias, pouring water over Ciro's wounds, catching the runoff with the ruined shirt. The gouges from the kanaima's claws ran across his chest from shoulder to sternum, splitting the skin. The wounds were long and bloody but didn't appear too deep, and Ayelen swallowed back the bile that rose at the thought of how much worse they might have been. Matias raced back toward her, stumbling as he neared, and for a moment, she worried he'd fall. Catching himself on a branch, he tossed her the bottle of alcohol.

Ayelen caught the bottle and took the clean shirt from him. "Now is hardly the time for acrobatics."

"Well, I wouldn't be me if I didn't try." He gave her a tight smile.

She hesitated, uncertain if what she was about to do was right, and her attempt at levity hadn't helped. She'd only ever seen it done before and hadn't ever officially been instructed.

Matias set his hand on her shoulder. "I'll hold him down for you," he said with a choked voice. With a sympathetic smile, he squeezed her shoulder. She smiled back. A hug would have set her to tears, and she there was no time for that now.

"I'm so sorry, *mi amor*, but this is going to hurt."

"More than it already does?" Ciro managed a half-smile, his eyes still tight with pain. "I can hardly imagine that."

"Can you sit up a bit?"

"For you, I would fight demons," Ciro said while Ayelen helped him. "Or even a crazy man in a jaguar skin."

Matias took his place behind Ciro, bracing his arms, and set a bit of wood and cloth into Ciro's mouth. Ayelen stood beside her brother and pulled off the blood-soaked shirt. She held the bottle of alcohol over his chest and paused, her own heart pounding.

"Are you ready?" she asked.

The sarcastic look he gave her was almost enough to steel her nerves. Taking a deep breath, she poured the drink across his chest. His muffled scream tore at her heart as he pushed against her brother. Finally, it was finished, and she tore the clean shirt into strips, wrapping it around his chest and tying it off. Ayelen set Ciro's arm in a sling to keep him from moving it and reopening the chest wounds.

Shaking, Matias helped Ciro remove the gag, then moved away to relight the fire.

Spirits of my fathers, protect my husband. Ayelen sent a prayer to Jepira and began the warding ritual against evil spirits. She walked in a circle around her husband, taking in and spitting out mouthfuls of the alcohol to guard her injured husband. When she finished, she wrapped the blanket over her husband's shoulders and curled up beside him in the hammock.

He wrapped his good arm around her and leaned his head back, his breathing shaky but steady. She lay with her head on his unwounded shoulder, wishing she could do more to help him with the pain. As she relaxed, a shudder tore through her. Once she had begun shaking, she found she could not stop.

Ciro pulled her closer, kissing the top of her head. "It's all right now," he whispered hoarsely. "I'll be fine. We'll all be all right."

She nodded and focused on her breathing, trying to make the trembling subside. The kanaima had been more foul than she could have imagined. She had been an utter fool to go after it alone. But then again, the Dream had told her that she must, or everyone she loved would die. Seeing that man-creature over her husband, ready to tear him down, had been the most frightening thing in her life. She couldn't imagine how it had been for Ciro to face its cold, white eyes. And yet ...

Ayelen's mind stuttered at the realization. And yet, she had stared it down. Twice it had looked right at her. And somehow had not seen her. Her hand dropped down to her belly. The kanaima never killed infants. Because it could not see them. It had looked right at her and not seen her.

Hope threatened to fill her, and she had to know for sure. She threw her consciousness into the Dream World as fully as she could while awake. In the distance, she could sense the miasma coming from the kanaima, but for now she ignored it. She ran her hands across her belly, searching. And there it was. A tiny bit of light, no larger than her thumbnail. How long had it been there and she hadn't noticed?

Hello, my daughter.

The light that was her daughter radiated love back to her, and for a moment Ayelen was filled with joy.

"Sister," Matias hissed from the waking world, dragging her back to her body as he shook her shoulder. "Wake up. We need to move."

Coming to, Ayelen sat up, blinking the lingering fuzziness of the Dream World from her eyes.

"I've packed the horses — everything but your hammock here. We need to find a safe place to rest until Ciro is strong enough to make the journey home."

Ayelen nodded her agreement, woke Ciro, and explained the situation to him. How would she tell him he was finally going to be a father? He would be overjoyed. She took down the hammock while Matias helped Ciro to his horse. A child changed everything. Where before she had only her own life to think about, now there was another. A daughter who would be entirely dependent on her and Ciro. Her entire life would hinge on the decisions they made.

Ayelen swung up onto her horse and allowed Matias to lead them, Ciro in the middle. Perhaps Ciro had been right to insist they go to Spain. Matias led them to a small cave and had her wait with the horses while he kindled a fire at the mouth and swept the corners with a torch, cleaning out as much of the wildlife as possible. Once he declared himself satisfied, she made up a bed for her husband to rest on while Matias helped him off the horse.

Together, Ayelen and her brother set up the makeshift camp while Ciro rested. His gentle snores were a small addition to the noise of the wildlife as brother and sister sat across from each other beside the fire, chewing on dried goat meat. In the morning, they would return like Ciro had suggested, gather some warriors, and let them take care of the kanaima.

"You can't go back," Matias said, as though he'd been reading her mind.

"Ciro was right, though. I'm no match for that thing." Without thinking, she laid her hand protectively over her flat belly.

Matias nodded with a sigh. "I suspected as much when it didn't see you. You're the only one who can free the man from the demon, and you can do it without risking your life."

"Don't tell Ciro, not yet." She glanced back at her sleeping husband. "I don't want him to worry."

"What is there to worry about? The thing won't even know you're there."

Ayelen shook her head. "You've got it backwards. It's not the demon jaguar riding the man's soul. It's the man himself. He's captured the jaguar and is using it like … some sort of parasite. It's the jaguar that clouds his eyes. Once they're separated, I will have no more protection from him than any other woman from an evil man. If I try to do this alone, it will kill me."

"How many others will die if you don't? You are here now. You know where it is, you know it is wounded, you have a better idea than anyone of how to destroy it. If not you, then who?"

Ayelen turned her head away. How could he understand how her world had shifted, meeting her daughter the way she had? Nothing in the world seemed more important right now than protecting her small family.

"What of all your talk about being Zyanya?" Matias said softly. "Did that mean so little to you that you'd throw it to the mud the moment you have a tough decision to make?"

11

PAIN CLAWED AT Ciro's chest when he came to, the smell of woodsmoke in the air around him. The voices of his family spoke softly not too far away. He loved the sound of his wife's voice, even when she was upset. The more he focused on her words, the easier it became to push the sharp pain aside.

"You're Zyanya as much as I, Matias. Why aren't you the one stepping up to protect your family?"

Yes, my friend, why haven't you been you? Would Matias tell his sister what he'd told no one else? Ciro opened his eyes to watch the exchange.

"Because I'm a coward, that's why. You're the one with all the fire."

"Nonsense," she said. "You're here, aren't you?"

Matias scoffed. "Only because I was dragged here." His shoulders slumped. "I wouldn't have come otherwise. I only get in the way, and I ..."

Ayelen moved closer to her brother and put her arm around his shoulder. "You're not worthless, and I'm glad you're here."

He shrugged her off. "But I froze, each time. When you really needed me, I couldn't help."

"You stopped me from chasing after the kanaima when it went for Ciro, and—"

"I didn't!" He cut her off, pushing her away and standing. He ran his fingers through his hair and paced. "I couldn't hold on. The moment you first struck me, I nearly let you go. Every time. *Every* time, it's all I can do to keep from vomiting. Except I can't, because my throat closes off, too, and I can't breathe. I can't think. Sometimes I can't even see."

Ciro watched him pace, stunned.

Ayelen shook her head. "Is it an injury? If you're hurt—"

"No." He cut her off again, bitterness coloring his voice. "It's not an injury. Not a physical one, anyway. I'm just a coward. I can't get past it. Every time, I'm just back *there*, my guts crawling with the fear. And there's no way to fight back, no escape, nothing but the *pain*, and it doesn't end …"

Ayelen reached out to him. "You're not a coward, Matias."

He turned away from her and crossed his arms over his chest, and Ayelen dropped her arm. "I should be able to push it away. To ignore it, to overcome it. But I just don't ever want to feel pain like that again." Matias's voice broke. "And so I am useless."

Ciro's heart broke, hearing his brother-in-law's confession. And he had done nothing to help. Instead, he had only pushed Matias forward, concerned with

Matias only when it interfered with his own goals. Shame washed over him, and he tried to sit up, desperate to apologize to his friend.

"You're not useless, Matias. You never have been, and you never will be. I couldn't have helped Ciro on my own today."

"If I hadn't held you back, maybe you could have killed the thing instead of only injuring it. I couldn't even watch. I was too busy hiding like a baby." Matias's voice filled with false cheer as he hid behind his smile. "Maybe that's why it didn't see me. I'm not enough of a man to be worth its time."

"Matias." Ayelen shook her head.

"Looks like you're more of a man than I am," he said, gently punching her arm. "Even pregnant."

"What?" Ciro's voice creaked in his dry throat.

Startled, Matias and Ayelen both turned toward him.

"How ... how long?" Ciro pushed through the pulling discomfort of his bandaged injuries and worked himself to sitting. His tongue felt full and swollen in his parched mouth, and the world shifted crazily for a moment before he found his bearings. They would have a child. A daughter, if old Nana was to be believed. How long had Ayelen known?

Ayelen glanced at her brother before moving to sit beside Ciro. She set her hand atop his and leaned gently against him. "I only just realized it, *mi amor*. It's still very early."

He rested his hand on her flat belly as images rose to mind. The way she would look, heavily pregnant, no doubt radiant and smiling. Holding their precious child in her arms. Holding his daughter in his arms. Something deep within Ciro shifted at the thought of the precious, tiny human — *a daughter* — who would be entirely dependent on his protection. At the idea that he would be more responsible for this little child they had created together than he'd ever been for anything in his life. He rocked back with the emotion of it and looked to Ayelen. She smiled warmly at his expression and hugged him.

"Nothing bad will ever happen to her, *mi amor,* so long as I live," he whispered, holding his wife close, ignoring the searing pain across his chest. But it brought his mind abruptly back to the where and why they were there, and he pulled away. "You were right. This thing needs to be stopped before it hurts anyone else."

Ciro took her hands between his, hoping she would see reason now. "But you must go back to the village." He held tightly when she tried to pull away and spoke before she could protest. "If not for yourself, then for the child you now carry. I heard you two talking. That monster is hurt; right now is the best chance anyone is going to have to kill it. But you're not just risking your own life any more, Ayelen. If she'd been born, would you have carried our infant daughter on your back to do this thing or left her someplace safe?"

To his surprise, tears filled her eyes. Bewildered, he released her hands. He had made her angry plenty, but he'd never before made her cry. "What's wrong?"

She shook her head and stood, her voice thick with emotion. "I need to get you some water. I'll be back."

"What did I say?" Ciro looked from his wife's retreating figure, as she nearly ran from the cave, to Matias's thoughtful face.

"You agreed with her."

"Then why is she crying?" Many times in his life, Ciro had thought he understood women, but every time it had simply been the universe toying with him. He'd thought for sure this time he understood them, or at least understood her. But here again, he found himself so incredibly wrong. Why couldn't they just act sane once in a while?

Matias sighed and dropped down beside the fire, across from Ciro. "She's crying because it hurts. You have both wanted this child so deeply, and for so long, and now that you have it, you both want to protect it, to the extent that you would give nearly anything to do so. If you asked her to, I think she would go with you right this moment to Spain."

"Then why—"

Matias cut him off with a wave of his hand. "She would go with you, but she would hate you and despise herself for the rest of her life. Can you really ask that of her? To break faith with everything she believes in? She is here and can stop the slaughter of so many lives. But at what price? She must choose between two opposing truths that have equal claim on her heart. One holds only the risk of death, for herself, for you, and possibly for your child, but the reward of so many lives. The other holds certain destruction for her soul and the guilt of all the dead that may follow." Matias shrugged, snapping a twig in two. "Which would you have her choose?"

"Neither," Ciro said firmly. "You and I together can hunt the thing tonight, while she remains safe here. There is no need to put her into further danger."

"I cannot go with you, *waré*. And before you suggest it, I can't even stay here to protect her." Matias tossed the broken bits of wood into the flames.

"I don't believe that for an instant, brother." Ciro moved to lean back against the wall of the cave. "I heard some of what you said to her, and I agree with her. You are far from useless."

Matias gave Ciro a sad smile across the flames. "There existed a time, once, when I believed so, too. I was young then, full of myself, believing I could do good in the world. One evening, as I walked along the streets of Maracaibo, enjoying the rare moment to myself between the work for my father, I saw several men fall on a boy not much younger than myself. They beat him, cursing his mestizo blood, and dragged him into an alley. And I, knowing so clearly what was good and right and what was not, went to intervene."

Ciro listened in silence, his heart heavy while he listened to Matias's story, knowing already how it would end. But Matias needed to lance the wound that festered in his soul, and Ciro feared that if he so much as moved, his friend would again close up.

"It was great foolishness." He shook his head, his lips tight. "Instead of helping, I only made things worse for the both of us. The men turned on me." He shuddered and crossed his arms, as though holding himself together. "They bound me, beat me, and when they had finished with me, they threw me on the floor where I could watch them do the same to the boy. I watched him die by their hands but was too broken to try to stop them. Too afraid to draw their attention back to me." Matias met Ciro's eyes. "The thing is, if I had only turned aside, they probably would have let him live."

Ciro wanted to reassure him that the fault wasn't his, but he couldn't find the words that would help Matias really understand. Everything he thought of felt flat and unreal in the face of his friend's pain.

"As punishment for my foolishness and cowardice in the moment, the gods have decided that I am to relive it every chance I get. Every time anyone even bumps me, for a moment I am back there, being slammed against the wall. I hear someone cry out in pain, and it is my own scream filling my ears, begging them not to kill me. My own sister hits my gut, and I am there, tasting the blood in my mouth as I lie helpless, watching that boy die again and again and again. I cannot protect her, Ciro." Matias put his hand up to the flames, waving it slowly through the smoke. "I left something of myself in the alley. I try to pretend that I didn't, but it is gone, and I am not."

12

AYELEN STOOD IN THE darkness outside the small cave, listening to her brother's story, the canteen of water held close to her chest. Why hadn't he trusted her with this? She would have understood. She would have listened without judgment and stood between him and anyone who would have dared to harm him. But then again, perhaps that was what he'd been trying to avoid.

"Matias." Ciro's deep voice sounded clear and soft in the night, and Ayelen watched the firelight move across the ground before her. "I can't say that I understand entirely what you've gone through, but I can say that you are no coward. You know, better than any of us, what horrors you'll relive each time you do something, and yet you still try. You ran to help when the kanaima first attacked the village. You came with me to find your sister, *despite* your fear. And not once, but twice, you held her back, even though you knew your personal repercussions. That is not cowardice, my brother, but true bravery."

In that moment, Ayelen found she loved her husband even more than she already had, for comforting her brother, for reaching him when she could not.

"It is not bravery to cower in fear, nor to run the other way when danger threatens those you love." The bitterness in his voice made her want to weep.

"I can't change how you feel about yourself. But know that, without reservation, I will always call you brother. And if you cannot believe it of yourself, you can cling to the knowledge that I will always consider you one of the bravest men I know."

"Even if I leave?"

There was a pause, and a sound as though Ciro had moved across the ground. "It takes as much courage to do what needs to be done, even if that means accepting that sometimes you cannot help. I will still love you, my brother, even if you leave."

Tears pushed against Ayelen's eyes, and she waited a moment, afraid to embarrass them with her eavesdropping. A weight settled into her stomach, and she rested her hand on her belly. If Matias could suffer through his trials with a smile in order to do his duty to his people and his family, how could she do any less? *I'm sorry, my daughter, but it is what must be.*

Clearing her throat and making some scuffling noises on the ground to give warning, Ayelen moved into the cave. Perhaps she could send him back without shame.

"I've been thinking, Matias. If you go back for reinforcements, perhaps Ciro and I can continue tracking the kanaima." She handed Ciro the canteen and met his eyes. He nodded slightly and drank. Afraid he would see the pity in her eyes, she looked away from her brother as she spoke. "Go saddle your horse while I make you a pack."

Matias rose without speaking and went out.

"We have to do this, *mi amor*." She knelt beside him, her back to the cave entrance.

"I know." Ciro tucked a strand of hair behind her ear. "But let me do the dangerous part. Perhaps if we can find him, I can lure him out, and you, staying some place out of sight and safe, can work your magic."

"I could help you fight him. He won't even know I'm there."

"No, please." Ciro shook his head, hiding the pain from his wounded shoulder. If she saw how much he hurt, she would never agree to stay behind. "I wouldn't be able to concentrate on fighting if I knew you were in danger. Please?"

Ayelen bowed her head. "All right, we'll try it your way."

13

Matias lifted the saddle onto his horse, listening to the quiet voices of his sister and her husband. Despite everything, hearing them speak like that, their voices full of love, always made him smile. Perhaps, some day, he really would find someone who accepted him, flaws and all. But it wouldn't be here. They had shown him kindness, a way out of the pain he was in, by letting him run messages. But that was a thing for children, and it stung his pride, what was left of it. Despite their words of comfort, they, too, did not see him as a man.

A noxious scent blew across him, and he wrinkled his nose, patting the horse on its neck. "That is some impressive gas you've passed there, my friend."

The horse snorted, restless, and Matias moved to its head, cooing. "Calm down." He pulled the bridle, lowering the animal's head, but instead of calming, it reared, striking Matias in the chest. Pain seared across his ribs and chest, and for a moment, he couldn't breathe as he fell to the ground and rolled out of the way of the horse's descending hooves.

The rank scent grew, and fear stole into Matias's heart as he gasped for breath through the sharp pain. The kanaima.

It was here.

Matias stilled beneath the foliage as it neared, the horses shrieking in fear. The thing walked passed them, no more than a handbreadth from Matias. It moved, cat-like, through the trees. The jaguar pelt covering its head seemed to snarl, and a tail of blackness flicked by. And there, glowing with a pale green light across the creature's chest, lay the necklace of pink *tu'uma* interspersed with the jaguar's claws. The kanaima smiled, baring his horrible teeth in the vicious smile of joy in violence.

Matias closed his eyes against the barrage of his senses, but he could not stop the sensation of being back in the alley, his tormentors smiling that same horrible smile while they worked to destroy him.

Matias. A voice of calm reached for him, but he pulled into himself more tightly.

Matias, you must destroy the necklace.

No, I'm leaving. The memory of each hit struck him again. The foul stench of the kanaima brought to mind the sickly smell of blood on the stones.

You must destroy the necklace, or far more than the three of them will die. The fate of all the Wayuu lies in your hands, son of Zyanya.

I can't. But even as he thought it, he felt calm hands touch his head, easing the pain, and guiding him to his feet.

Can't, or won't? He could not tell if the thought was his or not. The pain in his chest stabbed at him with each breath, and a rattle spread under his ribs. "Neither," he whispered, pulling out his knife.

14

A SHOUT MADE AYELEN turn, jerking toward the cave entrance, but as she did so, something large hit her, knocking her to the ground. She struck the rock and pain shot through her skull. Abruptly, she found herself in the Dream World, standing over her unconscious body. She watched, unable to help, as the kanaima leapt onto Ciro.

Fear filled her, freezing her in place while Ciro brought his good arm up in defense against the creature. They landed in a tangled heap, and Ayelen held her breath, too shocked to even pray. Ciro shoved the kanaima off of him and reached for his sword.

Move, fool girl! The voice of command rang in her ears, and she started. She needed to get back into her body to help him. She tried to wake but could not. Her head pounded, and she knelt beside her body. Blood had begun to pool behind her head. No wonder it ached, but her body still breathed. She wasn't dead yet.

Determined, she turned back to the kanaima. The creature was even more fierce in the Dream World than it appeared in the waking one. In the Dream World, the man fought, half crazed, with knife-like claws coming from his hands. The jaguar lay tethered to the man's back, tied along his body so that each physical blow of the kanaima was strengthened by the jaguar's soul. The jaguar roared its fury, its pain and anger at being so used, and the man channeled it into each strike.

Without further thought, Ayelen ran to them. A knife made of spirit stuff formed in her hand, and she began cutting at the ropes that bound the jaguar's soul. With each stroke, another tether appeared, cutting into the animal's dark fur.

Faster, she hissed to herself. She needed to be faster, to cut them before they could grow back. Broadening her strokes and sharpening her knife with a thought, she moved along the lines of the dance, her feet pounding out the familiar rhythm, stepping in just the right way to move alongside the fighting spirit as it continued its attack on her husband. A single stroke upward split the link between the jaguar's hind leg and the man's right. The kanaima sagged on a suddenly weakened knee, and Ciro kicked at it.

The next stroke fell downward, running along the man's right arm, severing the ties to the jaguar's forelimb. The loss of the jaguar's strength weakened the kanaima's deathblow, and Ciro blocked it, knocking it away and kicking the off-balance creature away from him.

Ayelen moved for a third strike along the jaguar's side as the kanaima stumbled backward, tripping over her still form. The pain of his weight landing across her legs jarred her, and her stroke fell short. The kanaima scrambled to its feet while Ciro lunged forward with his sword. The creature kicked Ayelen's legs out of its way viciously.

The pain threatened to pull her back to consciousness and she couldn't help but groan.

Ciro faltered just a moment at the sound. But a moment was enough for the kanaima.

No! She screamed as the kanaima got past Ciro's guard and slashed at him again. She jumped atop the kanaima's spirit form and hacked ruthlessly at the linkages as Ciro's body hit the ground. Why wouldn't they stop relinking?! She needed to be faster.

The kanaima turned slowly from its fallen prey and looked to what had caused it to stumble. As Ayelen hacked at the linkages to the thrashing jaguar, the eyes of the kanaima cleared. In a moment of understanding, she realized it knew she was there. The jaguar might not have been able to infer her presence in the negative space, but the man could.

Kneeling, the kanaima felt its way up her body to her neck. She could feel its cold, clawed hands grasping her throat, cutting off the air to her lungs. In defiance, her heart beat faster. The world around her seemed to slow as she began again the fluid dance of cutting the bonds. But though she moved as fast as thought, it was not enough.

The edges of the Dream World darkened around her, heightening in contrast at the same time.

Beyond the kanaima she could see her brother, knife in hand, running toward them.

No, brother, she tried to call out, but her voice was cut off. *It'll kill you, too.*

For a moment, the world around them paused, and Matias stood beside her in the Dream, smiling. *I know. But I do it for you.* He reached for the speck of light that lay against Ayelen's belly. *And for her. Be ready to move.*

The moment passed. Matias's body leapt through her spirit self and onto the kanaima's back, digging his knife at the creature's neck. The kanaima jerked backward, slamming Matias against the cave wall, but he clung on, searching for the necklace. Released from the kanaima's choking hold, Ayelen's body gasped for breath.

Matias's knife caught the leather strap of the necklace, and he jerked his hand upward, exposing his own ribs. Jaguar claws and bits of *tu'uma* scattered across the cave.

With a cry of triumph that echoed through the Dream World, the kanaima buried its knife into Matias's chest.

A scream of denial pressed itself through her, and she again went to work severing the jaguar's bonds. This time, they did not grow back.

Matias threw himself onto the kanaima, knocking it to the ground, his own knife sliding down behind the creature's collarbone as they fell.

The kanaima struggled to throw off Matias, gasping wetly for breath. It struck out frantically, as though it could fight off the certain death Matias's knife had delivered, again knocking Ayelen's battered, unconscious body across the ground. For a moment she hesitated, torn between returning to her body to protect it and freeing the jaguar. As she hesitated, Ciro crawled over to her. She could trust him to protect her. She turned back to the jaguar.

The jaguar growled at her, baring its teeth. What would happen to her if it attacked in the Dream World? What would happen to her daughter? She looked back to her body on the ground. Ciro had thrown himself between her and the dying monster. If she didn't sever the link, would the kanaima actually die? Centering herself, she turned back to the jaguar and dodged in for one final cut. With a single, swift motion, she severed the link from the kanaima's heart to the jaguar's.

The cat screamed in fury again, striking out blindly at whatever had caused it pain. Ayelen fell back, her arms protectively across her child. The jaguar leapt away from them both and ran a few paces before turning back to her. Its tail flicked back and forth. For a moment she feared it would leap on her. She met its eyes, waiting. Slowly, it blinked its yellow eyes, as though in acknowledgment if not actual thanks. She nodded, and it leapt away, disappearing into the Dream.

Now that's a lovely sight, don't you think? Matias asked, standing beside her.

She turned to him, startled to see him whole and well. She threw herself into his arms. *I thought you were lost!*

Naw, I've never been more sure of myself. He grinned at her, a smile of actual joy, with all the teasing silliness she remembered from their childhood. How she had missed that. The way it brightened his face seemed almost real.

I never knew you for a Dream Talker, she said, excited at the prospect of showing him the Dream World.

I'm not.

The words chilled her to the bone. In the waking world, Ciro bound her injuries and her body shuddered.

She shook her head. This ... this was not happening.

Matias looked away from her, to the North. *Can you hear them? They call me.*

Who?

Matias took a step forward and she reached out for his arm. He looked back at her kindly. *Father is calling for me. I hear Grandfather, too. They are waiting to take me to* Jepira.

Tears fell from her cheeks in the Dream World, mirrored by the very real tears that fell into the dirt beside her head. *Will I ever see you again?*

His smile turned sad for a moment, and he touched her shoulder. She looked down to see a dark claw mark along her chest. *Sooner than either of us would like, I think. But go now. You have time yet, and a daughter awaiting you. Live and be happy, and we will meet again.*

He hugged her one last time before turning to the North and disappearing into the forest.

15

CIRO SAT BESIDE his unconscious wife, carefully dripping broth onto her lips in the hope that she might swallow some. He had attended to her wounds; they all appeared minor. Even the bleeding on her head had seemed worse than it really was. As she'd slept, he had disposed of the corpse of the kanaima and wrapped his brother-in-law's body. They would need to carry it back to the village for a hero's burial.

He found, watching her, that all his plans and concerns about what *could be* had fallen away. All that mattered was that he be here, with her, right now. If she wanted to stay, they would.

"Anything you want, *mi amor*, is yours if you'll only come back to me," he whispered, kissing her hand. Ayelen stirred, and he watched. Hope, both painful and desperate, filled him. Perhaps this time, she would fully wake. After what felt like an eternity, she opened her eyes, and he let out a breath, his heart in his throat. He couldn't hold back his tears as he gathered her into his arms.

A DAUGHTER OF ZYANYA PREQUEL
Morgan J. Muir

Chapter 1

SPRING 1739 - MARACAIBO

MARIAH STOOD in the fading evening light of the pier beside her father, a gentle breeze teasing her long black hair. The floating villages on Lake Maracaibo began to light their evening lights, and in the western distance, the nightly thunderstorm gathered. The three other young women chatted with each other, but Mariah remained silent. Her heart lay heavy in her chest as she kept vigil over the body of her canine companion, friend, and protector.

Elisa had seen him first, just a squirming bundle of ears and paws in a sailor's rucksack. But it had been Mariah who had claimed both the pup and his heart.

Mariah had saved his life, and he had saved hers in return.

As the darkness gathered, the other girls draped garlands over their lost playmate and returned to their homes. The funeral had been their idea. As soon as they realized the extent of Alistair's injuries, her three friends had spent the last few days cheerily making fanciful funeral plans. The romantic and untraditional idea of sending him off to sea enthralled them. Mariah, however, had lain with her hound, draining herself of tears and doing all she could to ease his passing.

Mariah watched the small barge move out onto the lake, backlit by the distant lightning. Nothing would ever bring joy to her again. Her gaze remained fixed on the dark smudge. It danced along the surface of the water until she lost it among the twinkling lights of the native's floating homes. The lights seemed to watch her, their sympathy at her loss nearly as painful as her guilt. Her eyes blurred as she watched. She struggled to blink back the tears, but they ran down her face anyway. She jumped when her father rested his hand on her shoulder, and she wiped away the wetness from her cheeks before turning toward him. For a moment, looking up into his face, Mariah saw a depth in this man that went beyond just being her father.

The profound pain of loss that ached in her heart, loss of her dearest friend and confidant, she found reflected in his face. She knew, however, that his pain ran far deeper. He looked with unfocused eyes over the water. Perhaps he met the eyes of the natives who had come out to the edge of their *palafitos*, their floating village, to watch the strange ceremony. Perhaps he saw the ghost of her mother, whom Mariah had never known, her loss still so fresh and painful that he never spoke of her to his daughter. What life had her father, Don Ciro Álvarez Bosque, merchant and businessman, lived and known that Mariah knew nothing of? For the first time in her sixteen years of life, Mariah wondered who her father truly was.

She turned back to the water, hoping to again find the barge among the broken reflection of the waning moon. But it was no longer there. The two of them remained in silence, each consumed with their own thoughts in the inky darkness.

***

The moon glistened across the calm waves of the lake, its light blurred by the clouds as Michael walked beside the ship's rail. The texture of the hard wood flowed beneath his fingers like frozen waves, guiding his fingers along inevitable paths. Michael looked up from the water, with its floating lights, to the stern of the anchored merchant ship. The floating wooden beast had been his home for the past several months as they'd crossed the world. He snorted at the thought. It wasn't home; it was merely a place to exist. The abandoned helm called to him. He was meant to have captained a ship like this, a path that had lain before him as frozen and inevitable as the wood grain of the rail.

Or so he'd thought.

A warm breeze full of floral scents blew across the deck. It reminded him forcibly of old, vague memories full of warmth and honesty. Scowling, he pulled his gaze from the helm and crossed to the other side of the deck. He ought to turn in for the night. The morning would bring the typical hectic rush of work, offloading and reloading merchandise. Just another day of backbreaking labor, and then he'd be back to the sea.

The ocean called to him, as she did to every sailor. Entrancing, fickle. Beautiful and dangerous. She promised the freedom of salty wind in his face while under full sail, and the heady exhilaration of struggling for his ship's life along with his own whenever she felt tempestuous.

Michael snorted, leaning against the rail. Her promises were as empty and unfulfilling as her threats were full. He was just a toy for her to use for her own amusement, to be tossed aside when she was done. Not unlike certain captains.

Below him on the dock, movement caught his eye. He watched a small group of young women, gathered at the edge of a nearby pier, throw things onto a small barge. It had all the air of a funeral, but a shockingly small one. The barge was pushed out and Michael watched it pass his ship by. That would be his end. Serving this ship, or another like it, until the sea claimed him for her own.

Michael slammed his fist into the rail. He belonged to no one. Not this ship. Not the sea. Not his father's name.

The breeze again flowed over him, pulling at his dark hair. Tucking his loose hair back behind his ear, he turned away from the water. He needed to gather his things and get some sleep. It was time, and this place would be as good as any.

***

The smell of the water, full of life and potential, drifted over Mariah. The noise and bustle of the marketplace in the morning, punctuated by the cries of gulls in search of breakfast, were of little consequence as she moved toward the lake. Her friends followed behind her, their *duenna* trailing along some distance away, and Mariah listened to them with only half an ear.

"Did we have to come this way?" Selena asked with a sigh as she picked her way through the muddy, busy street.

"There was no reason not to," Betania said with her usual conciliatory manner.

"Except that you thought it a bad idea," Elisa pointed out. "And it would take longer. And—"

"Oh hush," Betania said to her sister. "I thought it might be nice, and Mariah wanted to come this way."

"Nice," Elisa muttered. "If you like the smell of fish guts." She swung her skirt to the side at the last minute to avoid brushing against a fishmonger's cart.

"You *would* think it's nice, Elisa," Mariah cut in, annoyed by Elisa's persistent whining. She would never understand why Betania's younger sister *always* had to follow along. "We all know it's your favorite perfume, but you could really learn to be more judicious about it."

Selena laughed, and Mariah knew Betania would be holding back her own laughter. Elisa would fume about it for a while and then try to come up with some cutting retort. The girl had actually begun to develop some real wit.

Not even a spark of amusement found its way into Mariah as they moved through the patchwork of sunlight and shadows. While Mariah's mind knew she should care—about something, anything—her soul simply didn't. She walked on, ignoring the chatter of her friends, and made her way to the pier. The glitter of the sun on the waves was the only thing bright; all else was muted. Dull.

The three other girls milled around her for a minute, forced by Betania to give her some time.

Elisa said something in a giggling whisper that Mariah didn't care enough to hear. Betania nudged Mariah out of her reverie and gestured discreetly to a young man walking down a nearby gangplank. He was tall, with dark hair, well dressed even if his clothes were a bit tattered, and he held a rucksack thrown over his shoulder. He looked out at the world with his head high and a grin, as if expecting something wonderful.

Mariah scowled. How could anyone be so cheery?

"Come on," she said, a flare of anger overcoming her apathy and spurring her into recklessness. Lifting her head, she led the girls deliberately toward him.

"What are you doing?" Betania whispered urgently. Poor, quiet Betania, always trying to take responsibility but too timid to succeed. Mariah took her arm firmly, and Betania fell into step.

"Seeing if Elisa can catch herself another salty puppy," Mariah said, just loud enough for the other two to hear.

Elisa and Selena stifled giggles, and Betania tightened her grip on Mariah's arm in disapproval but didn't try to stop her. Despite Mariah's efforts to not look as they passed, she couldn't help but notice the young sailor's gaze following them.

"Pardon me, señoritas," he called out, not even trying to hide his British accent.

Mariah grinned as she stopped the group.

"My name is Michael, and I'd be pleased to make the acquaintance of such lovely young women."

"He's all yours, Elisa," Mariah said, and the four of them turned back towards the sailor.

Elisa stepped forward with her hand outstretched, a sickeningly charming smile on her face and her golden hair shining in the sunlight. "I'm Elisa Díaz Palomo, daughter of Don Sergio Díaz Montejo, Señor de la Cuesta."

Elisa paused just long enough for the young man to take her hand and shake it. "This is my sister, Betania, my cousin, Selena Abano Palomo, and our dear friend, Mariah Álvarez Cordova." The girls curtsied as they were introduced, Betania and Selena both keeping their eyes modestly downward. "Welcome to Maracaibo, Miguel."

"Miguel. I like that." He released Elisa's hand and grinned. "*Merci*. It's not every day you're welcomed ashore by such visions of beauty. Might I walk with you for a bit, as we seem to be headed in the same direction?"

"What, away from the ship?" Mariah whispered to Betania, who stifled a laugh with a demure cough and a gloved hand, still pointedly studying the muddy road.

Elisa looked Miguel up and down, then cast a glance at her older sister, whose grip dug into Mariah's arm. Mariah shrugged, and Elisa held out her elbow for Miguel. "Certainly. We would be delighted!"

"Here," Mariah said, shifting Betania's death grip to Selena's arm as the group began forward. Shaking some feeling back into her own arm, Mariah slowed to look back at the lake. The water glimmered beyond the waiting ships, whispering beneath the cacophony of life about … something. It urged her aching heart to come to it. But her father had insisted that she get through today, and so she would. With regret, she turned from the water and caught up to her friends.

How much trouble might she get in for this bit of brashness? Her father would probably laugh, though

Doña Olivia would tighten her lips and use that disapproving tone. She could practically hear it now. *How dare you introduce yourself to some strange man! And a sailor at that. Surely you have better manners and care for your person. Blah blah blah.*

Mariah wrinkled her nose at the imaginary lecture. It wasn't as though they were in any real danger. The girls always had an escort, be it the Díaz girls' duenna—who currently looked as though she'd bitten into a lemon—or a member of the house staff. Especially now that Alistair was gone.

Mariah's throat tightened, and that stinging behind her eyes returned. She cut off that line of thought viciously, slamming the door shut on her melancholy. She wouldn't cry in public. Instead, she looked over Elisa's newest acquisition, determined to focus on something else. Anything else.

Miguel looked to be a couple years older than Mariah, seventeen or eighteen perhaps, tall and well built. Life at sea appeared to have treated him well; he had a healthy color and moved gracefully. For a moment, she wondered about his teeth; she hadn't noticed them before. But then again, it wasn't as though she was buying a horse. Mariah noted that he wasn't as broad as most men she had fancied, but he certainly wasn't bad to look at. If he was as young as she suspected, he would likely fill out in a couple more years, or so Nana always claimed of the young men her age.

He had dark hair, nearly as black as her own, which he wore pulled into a neat queue, tied at the nape of his neck. The loose sleeves of his white shirt billowed in the breeze and Mariah imagined his arms would be nicely muscled. His boots, though well made, were worn, as was his faded waistcoat. Given his build, apparent health, and fine-though-worn apparel, the chances were good he wasn't just a deckhand. Perhaps a junior officer? Mariah allowed herself a small grin as she imagined him fighting off pirates with the cutlass that swung at his hip.

Mariah listened for a moment to Selena and Betania's conversation. They were going on about the number of ships in the busy harbor and the weather out in the Gulf of Venezuela beyond the lake. They'd obviously spent too much time listening to their fathers go on about business. Not interested in that tedious topic—she got enough of it from her own father—she moved forward to walk beside Miguel. Looping his bag over his shoulder to free his unoccupied arm, he offered Mariah his elbow. Ignoring a moment of unease—this man was a stranger after all—she took his arm. He gave her a broad smile, and she smiled back at him, not caring that it didn't reach her eyes. Elisa shot her a withering look, which almost made Mariah's smile genuine.

"Miguel and I were just talking about where he is from," Elisa said with a careless flip of her golden hair.

"Actually—Mariah is it?—I was avoiding the subject of where I am from." He winked at her. "Speaking of which, Mariah, not Maria?"

Mariah rolled her eyes. "My mother was part French. As far as you go, it's obvious from your accent that you're British, though your Castilian seems decent. You've also employed a smattering of French, so I'm sure you've dealt with them as well."

"And what would you conclude from that?" he asked.

"I'm willing to bet that you've travelled the world. So tell us, mighty traveler, what have you seen?"

Miguel slowed to a stop, and she could practically feel Elisa's chagrin as he looked at Mariah. Mariah turned to him, and their eyes met, his green eyes capturing her. A few seconds, or perhaps an eternity, later Miguel broke contact, and they began forward again.

"Well," he began slowly, not looking at either of them, "I'm not really sure where I was born; somewhere in England, I'm told. My first memories are of being on a ship with my father, large as life, before me. I suppose I've travelled the world; it certainly feels like it. The last several years, I've mostly sailed the waters of Britain, France, and Spain. I have made the trip to India and back once. My father once told me that I'd even seen the Orient, though I don't really remember it."

While Elisa gave him her rapt attention, Mariah opted to look him over more closely, as much as she could without being obvious. He had a finely shaped face, with lively eyes lined with dark lashes, and a very expressive mouth. He looked like the type of person who enjoyed laughing. *No,* she thought to herself, *Elisa can have him.*

"Anyhow," Miguel continued, "after finally coming to the New World, I think I've had just about enough traveling. Perhaps I'll stay on for a while, especially if life here is as sweet as the señoritas."

Elisa and Mariah both blushed, but Mariah regained her tongue first.

"If you are going to stay here you're going to need more of a name than just Miguel," Mariah said.

"What's wrong with Miguel?" Elisa demanded, swinging forward to glare at Mariah.

"Yes, please enlighten me, fair lady." Miguel disentangled himself from Elisa and gave Mariah a mock bow. "What is wrong with my name?

Mariah laughed lightly. "Nothing. I think Miguel is a fine name. You just seem to have misplaced your surname."

"Drat. I knew I left something on that ship." Miguel feigned consternation. "Should I go back and fetch it?"

"Perhaps if you just called to it, it would come." Elisa joined in the play and rethreaded her arm through his.

"Hmmm ... It may be surly about being left behind. Perhaps if you angels attempted to call it."

Giggling, Elisa said, "Blanco!"

At the same moment, Mariah spoke up with "del Mar."

"Whoa, señoritas, one at a time, please! Let's see, Elisa suggests Blanco, and Mariah gives del Mar. What fine names for a man like me." He rolled his shoulders as though trying on a new coat. "They seem comfortable enough. I shall keep them both."

Elisa giggled yet again, and Mariah just shook her head at the silliness. The warehouses had given way to the two-storied buildings of rock and stucco. A crossroads marked the edge of town, beyond which the buildings sat further apart, their boundaries marked by fences and the occasional palm tree. Miguel stopped, bowing again to the girls.

"Well, ladies, I'm afraid this is where we must part."

"I hope to see you again soon." Elisa batted her eyes at him, and Mariah groaned. The girl was only fourteen, and was about as subtle as a brick to the head.

"I would like that very much. Casa de la Cuesta, right? I will surely call on you there." Miguel gave Elisa a most charming smile, too charming for Mariah, but Elisa soaked it in. "In fact, I look forward to seeing all of you again." He shook each of their hands in turn. "Elisa, Betania, Selena. Mariah."

Miguel held on to Mariah's hand a moment longer than the others'. In a quiet voice meant only for her, Miguel added, "Especially you, Mariah."

The other three girls started down the road while Mariah stood there in a sort of shock, heat rising into her face. No one had ever been so forward with her before. He gave her a sheepish grin, breaking the spell, and she turned away to catch up with her friends. As they strolled away, a gaggle of gossiping, giggling geese, Mariah looked back to see Miguel still standing where they'd left him, looking thoughtful.

"Miguel!" she called back as a mischievous feeling stole over her. He looked up and she continued, "Miguel, there's a merchant's office in town, just around the corner. There's pink coxcomb under the windows. You can't miss it. If someone were looking for employ, he might start there."

"I'll keep that in mind," he called back, raising his hand in farewell. "*Gracias!*"

She hurried back to her friends, looking back just before passing around a bend in the road. He still stood as they had left him. Finally, he hoisted his pack and turned back the way they had come.

AURA of DAWN
Available now on Amazon.com

Thank you for reading Guardian!

If you enjoyed reading Guardian, please consider leaving a review! It doesn't matter where—Amazon, Goodreads, Bookbub, or your own social media
Reviews are like gold to an indie author, and they buoy my spirits and stoke the fires of creativity.

NEED MORE DAUGHTER OF ZYANYA?

You can find the rest of the series on Amazon

Aura of Dawn – a Prequel
Amaranth Dawn – Book 1
Aeonian Dreams – Book 2
Abiding Destiny – Book 3

ABOUT THE AUTHOR

Morgan J Muir fell in love with reading fantasy as child, and could never get enough of it. She is a mom of three crazy kids and lives in northern Utah.
You can find more of her stories at morganjmuir.com

Made in the USA
Middletown, DE
18 September 2022